THE LEGEND

It all began a long time ago . . . Okoto was a peaceful and vibrant place. The island was split into six different realms, each ruled by a different element and tribe. Its inhabitants lived in harmony with one another, respecting other tribes and sharing the joy of life . . .

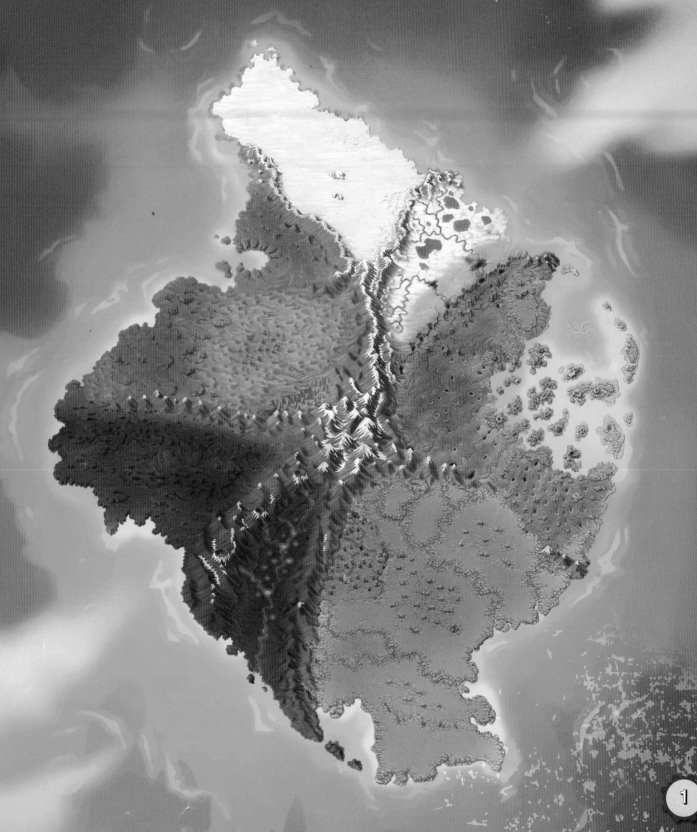

THE MASK MAKERS

Two brothers, Makuta and Ekimu, used six elements from Okoto Island to create Masks of Power for its inhabitants. They had one mask each. Makuta wore the Mask of Control, and Ekimu wore the Mask of Creation. Find all the MASKs the brothers made in the grid.

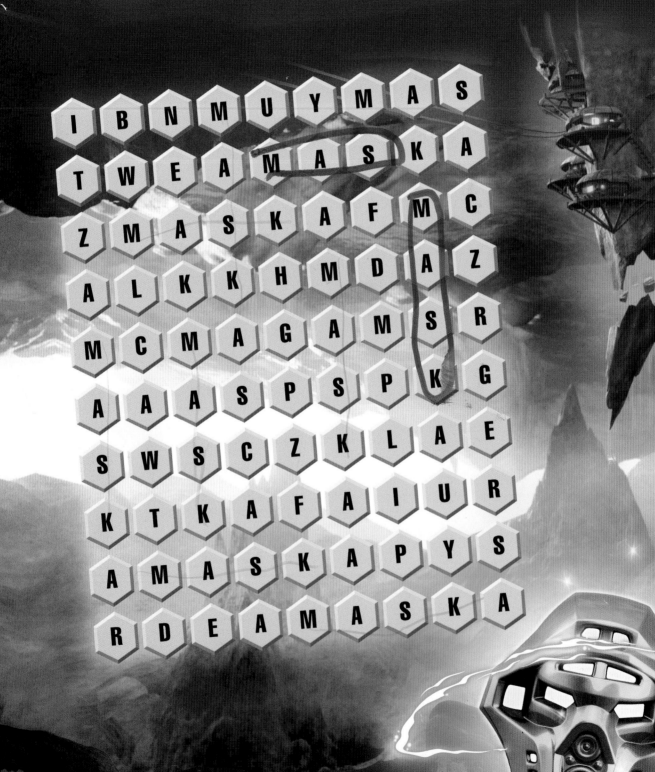

THE MASKS OF POWER

The masks created by the ancient mask makers had different properties and shapes, but the method to make them was always the same. Put your mask close to the shapes on the page. The matching ones will tell truths about the Masks of Power and their creators.

2.
Makuta made the Mask of Creation for himself.

1.
One Mask of Power could only contain the might of a single element.

5.
Nobody was mighty enough to wear the Mask of Ultimate Power.

3.
Ekimu was much better at making masks than his brother.

4.
The powerful Mask of Time belonged to Ekimu.

THE LEGEND

A LONG TIME AGO, ON THE MYTHICAL ISLAND OF OKOTO, ALL LIVED IN PEACE AND HARMONY.

FROM THE ISLAND'S ELEMENTAL FORCES, TWO BROTHERS, KNOWN AS THE MASK MAKERS, CREATED MASKS OF POWER.

EACH BROTHER HAD A SPECIAL MASK. MAKUTA HAD THE MASK OF CONTROL . . .

. . . AND EKIMU — THE MASK OF CREATION.

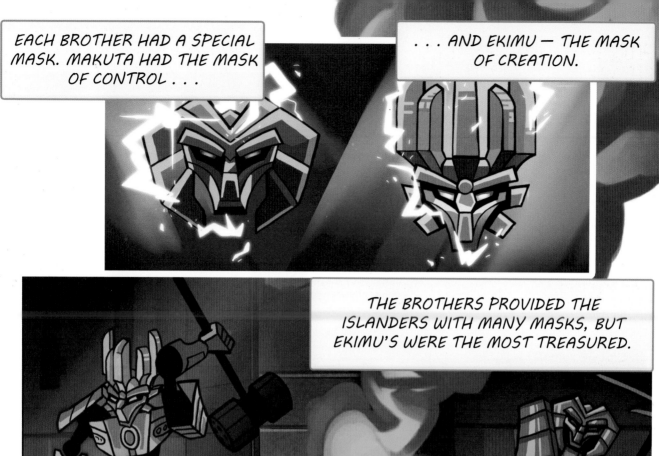

THE BROTHERS PROVIDED THE ISLANDERS WITH MANY MASKS, BUT EKIMU'S WERE THE MOST TREASURED.

HIS BROTHER BECAME ENVIOUS AND FORGED AN EVIL PLAN.

A SACRED LAW SAID THAT NO MASK COULD CONTAIN MORE THAN ONE POWER ELEMENT, OTHERWISE IT COULD BECOME TOO DANGEROUS.

BUT MAKUTA MADE THE STRONGEST MASK OF ALL TIME . . . THE MASK OF ULTIMATE POWER.

WHEN MAKUTA PUT IT ON, IT TOOK CONTROL OF HIM . . .

. . . AND THE ISLAND BEGAN TO SHAKE AND CRUMBLE!

REALIZING WHAT HIS BROTHER HAD DONE, EKIMU MANAGED TO KNOCK THE MASK FROM MAKUTA'S FACE.

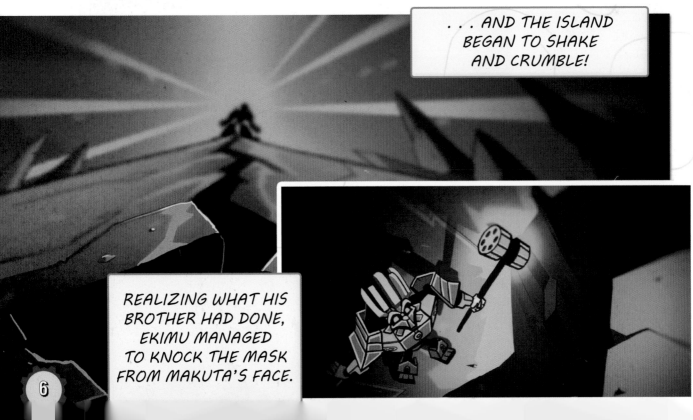

THEN, A SHOCK WAVE ROLLED ACROSS THE LAND AND SENT BOTH BROTHERS INTO AN ENDLESS SLEEP.

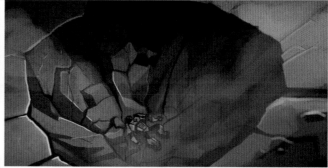

THE MASKS WERE SCATTERED ALL OVER THE ISLAND, WAITING FOR A TIME WHEN SOMEONE WOULD COME LOOKING FOR THEM . . .

SPIDER PLAGUE

The inhabitants of Okoto Island were attacked by Skull Spiders! These foul beasts were sent there by their master to find all the masks. Find and mark two identical spiders in the swarm. Watch out for the sharp limbs of the skull beasts!

PROPHECY

The Protectors of the island foresaw that help would come from space, and the evil spiders would be defeated. Untangle the lines and find out which realm each Protector used to look after.

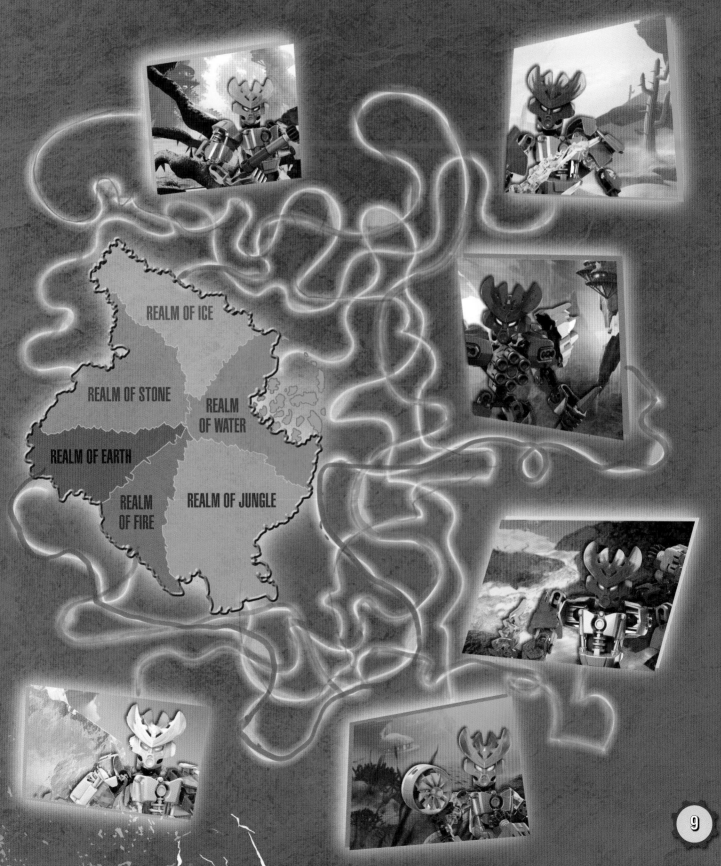

REALM OF ICE

REALM OF STONE

REALM OF WATER

REALM OF EARTH

REALM OF FIRE

REALM OF JUNGLE

THE HEROES ARRIVE

The prophecy was true — six Toa fell from the sky onto the island! Each landed in a realm connected with a different element. Help the islanders recognize their new guests! Match each Master with his or her description by drawing lines between them.

A

B

POHATU
1
The Master of Stone is great at throwing boomerangs and can turn into a wild tornado.

2
LEWA
The Toa of Jungle can fly. His weapons are two axes, which he skillfully wields even in dense forest.

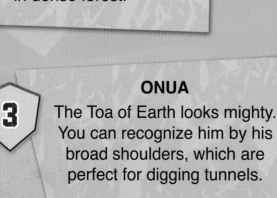

C

ONUA
3
The Toa of Earth looks mighty. You can recognize him by his broad shoulders, which are perfect for digging tunnels.

TAHU

The Toa of Fire owns two razor-sharp swords and loves gliding on his board across hot lava.

6

D

KOPAKA

He mastered fighting with a spear and a shield. This Master of Ice can also slide on icy slopes.

4

E

F

GALI

The Toa of Water feels at home in the deeps. The Skull Spiders will yield to the power of her trident.

5

THERE IS HOPE!

Now the Toa must find the six Masks of Power. The masks will help them combat the evil spreading on Okoto. Before embarking on this difficult journey, solve the puzzle of the ancients. Put the missing Masks of Power at the bottom of the page into the grid, so that none of them are repeated horizontally or vertically.

ICY JOURNEY

Kopaka and the Protector of Ice reached the heart of the white realm in search of the Mask of Power. It's hidden on a high mountain behind an icy labyrinth. Help the Toa of Ice cross the obstacle by drawing a line leading him straight to the mask.

START

FINISH

HEROIC DEFENSE

The Protector of Fire is preparing his defense as the Skull Spiders draw closer! Decipher the symbols near the attacking beasts and give the Protector the right shooting instructions. Help him defeat the spiders, so nothing disturbs Tahu from his task on the next page.

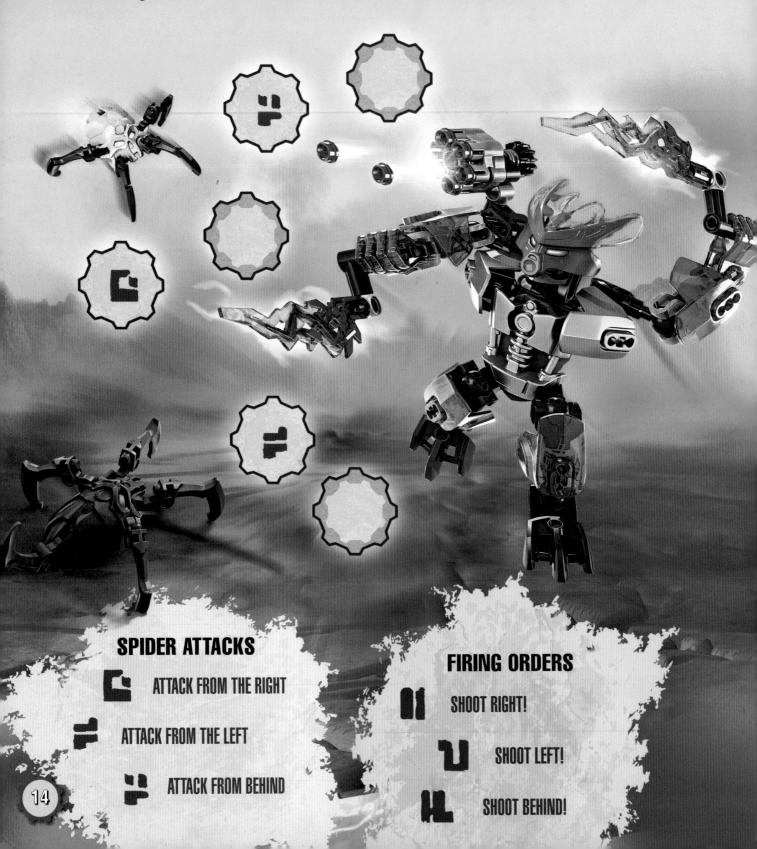

SPIDER ATTACKS

ATTACK FROM THE RIGHT

ATTACK FROM THE LEFT

ATTACK FROM BEHIND

FIRING ORDERS

SHOOT RIGHT!

SHOOT LEFT!

SHOOT BEHIND!

TOA OF FIRE

Tahu is sliding across the hot lava on his board. Can you finish the picture so he can reach the Mask of Fire? Write the numbers in the empty spaces. Be as quick as you can — the Toa is zooming!

A WEAPON WORTHY OF A TOA

The heroes are always weapon-ready — they never know when there might be Skull Spiders hiding just around the corner! Look at the Toa's equipment at the bottom of the page. Which of the six weapons is missing from the picture puzzles?

ROCK JUMPING

A huge underground cave hides the Mask of Power. The only way to reach it is by jumping on floating rocks. Onua can move from rock to rock only horizontally or vertically, and he may not step on the same rock twice!

 Jump on a rock next to the one you're on.

Jump on a rock that's two squares away.

DESERT TORNADO

In the Realm of Stone, at the heart of the desert, lies the Mask of Stone. Pohatu is as fast as a whirlwind and the Skull Spiders have no chance of stopping him from reaching it! Look at the scene and find ten differences between the two pictures.

JUNGLE TANGLE

The Jungle Realm is overgrown with dense forest and Lewa can barely see his Mask of Power in the thick vines.

Which three vines could he cut to get to the mask underneath?

UNDERWATER SIEGE

The Mask of Water is in danger! The Protector needs your help to defend it. Help her aim her torpedoes by drawing straight lines from each one so they stop as many Skull Spiders as possible.

LIMITED VISIBILITY

Deep underwater, Gali is searching for her Mask of Power. She has limited visibility so the mask is hard to see. Help the Master of Water spot the Golden Mask by finishing the drawing and coloring it in.

BATTLE IN THE ANCIENT CITY

WEARING THE NEW MASKS, THE TOA ARRIVED AT THE ANCIENT CITY OF THE MASK MAKERS IN THE HEART OF THE ISLAND OF OKOTO.

I THINK WE HAVE COMPANY!

A MONSTROUS SPIDER BARRED THE WAY TO THE CITY. IT WAS THE LORD OF SKULL SPIDERS WHO HAD COME TO TAKE THE TOA'S MASKS OF POWER!

THE HEROES MOVED TO ATTACK THE MONSTER.

AFTER A LONG AND GRUELING BATTLE THE LORD OF SKULL SPIDERS WAS DEFEATED . . .

. . . AND FELL FROM THE BRIDGE INTO A DEEP CHASM.

WHEN WE ACT TOGETHER, OUR MASKS HAVE THE POWER TO DEFEAT EVIL!

THE TOA ENTERED THE CITY TO LOOK FOR THE TOMB OF THE ANCIENT MASK MAKER.

WE MUST FIND EKIMU BEFORE THE ENEMY DOES! OUR MASKS WILL GUIDE US!

THE HEROES DID NOT KNOW THAT FIGHTING THE HORDES OF SKULL SPIDERS WAS JUST THE BEGINNING OF THEIR ADVENTURE . . .

BONY GUARDIANS

At the heart of the Ancient City lives the dark Skull Grinder. He sent two guardians to protect the path leading to Ekimu. Look at the ancient code from Okoto Island and use it to find the names of the Toa's new enemies.

AWAKENING

The Masters of Elements found the lost tomb, went inside, and woke the sleeping Ekimu. But this won't be the end of their struggle with evil forces. Look at the picture and connect each close-up with the right Toa.

GAME OF MASKS

The Skull Spiders stole the Fire Protector's mask! Embark on a dangerous journey with your friends to the heart of spider webs, and retrieve it. Who will reach the mask first? The rules are described on the next page. Before you begin, you must learn the rules of the game . . .

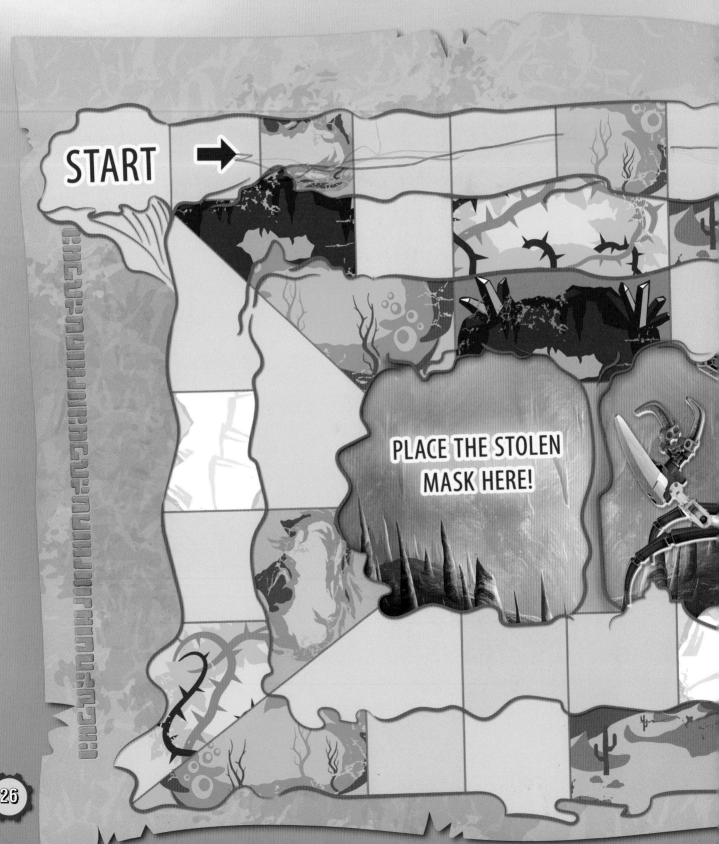

Rules:

Find some counters and a die. Each player must choose to be one of the six elements. Place your counters at the START. Take turns throwing the die and moving around the board. If your counter lands on the element you chose, you can roll again. When you reach the FINISH, you must defeat the powerful Skull Scorpio by rolling a 6. It is only then that you may collect the mask.

FINISH

QUIZ

The Toa retrieved all the Masks of Power! But this is not the end of their adventure, merely the beginning of their struggle against evil. Try to recall the events and answer all the questions below.

1 How many realms are there on Okoto Island?
A) 7
B) 6
C) 9

2 What were the names of the two brothers forging the Masks of Power?
A) Akido and Koda
B) Emiku and Maruka
C) Ekimu and Makuta

3 The mightiest mask, containing the power of all the elements was the Mask of . . .
A) Ultimate Power
B) Creation
C) Control

4 Which creatures attacked the inhabitants of Okoto?
A) snakes
B) scorpions
C) spiders

5 Who foretold the coming of the heroes?
A) The Patrons
B) The Protectors
C) The Premiers

6 Where did the six heroes come from?
A) They fell from the sky
B) They crawled up from under the ground
C) They stepped down from a magical mountain

7 What were the heroes called?
A) Tao
B) Toa
C) Toi

8 Fire, Water, Earth, Stone, Ice — which element master is missing?
A) The Master of Metal
B) The Master of Air
C) The Master of Jungle

9 Where did the Master of Stone, Pohatu, find his Mask of Power?
A) At the top of a rocky mountain
B) In the middle of a stony desert
C) In the stone pit

10 Tahu is the Master of . . .
A) Water
B) Fire
C) Earth

ANSWERS

p. 2
THE MASK MAKERS

I	B	N	M	U	Y	M	A	S
T	W	E	A	M	A	S	K	A
Z	M	A	S	K	A	F	M	C
A	L	K	K	H	M	D	A	Z
M	C	M	A	G	A	M	S	R
A	A	A	S	P	S	P	K	G
S	W	S	C	Z	K	L	A	E
K	T	K	A	F	A	I	U	R
A	M	A	S	K	A	P	Y	S
R	D	E	A	M	A	S	K	A

p. 3
THE MASKS OF POWER

1. One Mask of Power could only contain the might of a single element.

3. Ekimu was much better at making masks than his brother.

5. Nobody was mighty enough to wear the Mask of Ultimate Power.

p. 8
SPIDER PLAGUE

p. 9
PROPHECY

 REALM OF WATER

 REALM OF STONE

 REALM OF FIRE

 REALM OF JUNGLE

 REALM OF EARTH

 REALM OF ICE

pgs. 10–11
THE HEROES ARRIVE

A	B	C	D	E	F
4	6	1	3	2	5

p. 12
THERE IS HOPE!

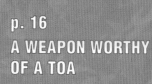

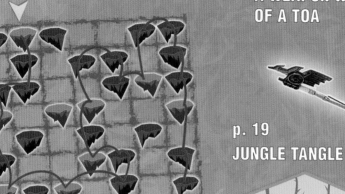

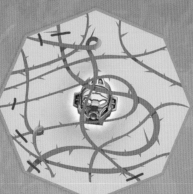

POHATU   LEWA   KOPAKA   ONUA   TAHU   GALI